My Sister the Supermodel

Look for more

titles:

#1 It's a Twin Thing
#2 How to Flunk Your First Date
#3 The Sleepover Secret
#4 One Twin Too Many
#5 To Snoop or Not to Snoop

TWO of a kind ™

My Sister the Supermodel

adapted by Megan Stine

from the teleplays written by
Tom Amundsen,
Bob Keyes & Doug Keyes

from the series created by
Robert Griffard
& Howard Adler

HarperEntertainment

A PARACHUTE PRESS BOOK

A PARACHUTE PRESS BOOK

Parachute Publishing, L.L.C.
156 Fifth Avenue
Suite 325
New York, NY 10010

Published by
HarperEntertainment
A Division of HarperCollins*Publishers*
10 East 53rd Street, New York, NY 10022-5299

For information address HarperCollins Publishers,
10 East 53rd Street, New York, NY 10022-5299.

ISBN 0-06-106576-5

First printing: August 1999

Printed in the United States of America

Visit HarperEntertainment on the World Wide Web at
http://www.harpercollins.com

10 9 8 7 6 5 4 3

CHAPTER ONE

"Ashley, you won't believe it! I have the most amazing news!" Jennifer Dilber called.

Ashley Burke whirled around to see her friend Jennifer rushing down the hall toward her. The last bell had just rung, and school was over. Ashley and her twin sister, Mary-Kate, were putting their books in their lockers.

"What?" Ashley asked, suddenly excited. Jennifer's eyes were growing wider every second.

It must be something big, Ashley thought.

"The Fashion Van is coming to our school!" Jennifer announced. "Isn't that absolutely fabulous? It's like they know I'm here!"

"What's a fashion van?" Mary-Kate asked.

Jennifer tossed her blond hair over her shoulders. She looked down her nose at Mary-Kate.

"Something you obviously don't know anything about," she said with a snooty smile.

"It's the guys from *Real Teen* magazine," Ashley explained to her sister. "They travel around to different schools and choose kids to appear in *Real Teen* magazine each month."

"Next week they'll be at our school to pick three girls. And they're going to choose me!" Jennifer squealed.

"Why do you think they're going to choose you?" Mary-Kate asked.

"Because they want only the most fashionable girls," Jennifer explained.

"Right." Mary-Kate nodded. "My point exactly. So what makes you think *you've* got a shot?"

Ashley glared at her sister. *Why does Mary-Kate always have to tease Jennifer?* she wondered. *Just because Jennifer and I are into clothes, boys, and shopping—and she's not?*

"What's her problem?" Jennifer snapped.

"Ignore her," Ashley told Jennifer. "My sister doesn't get *Real Teen* magazine. It doesn't come with a football T-shirt!"

"Very funny," Mary-Kate muttered.

"Isn't it perfect timing?" Jennifer went on. "Just when we were thinking about going to that Horizon School of Modeling."

"I know," Ashley agreed. "It's like fate!"

"But if you want to go to the model tryouts," Jennifer said, getting back to the main subject, "you've got to get a permission slip and have it signed by a parent. The slips are on the desk outside the main office."

"Come on," Ashley said, pulling her sister away. "I need one of those slips. And then we've got to get home—fast. This just might be the most important day of my life!"

"How do I look?" Ashley asked later that afternoon. She held her head up high and strutted through the front door as if she were walking on a model's runway.

Mary-Kate sighed and rolled her eyes. She threw her backpack on the couch.

Carrie, their young, hip baby-sitter, glanced up from the book she was studying at the dining table. She was a student at the college where the twins' father taught. Kevin Burke had hired Carrie to spend time with the girls while he was working. Ever since the twins' mother died three years ago, he had needed someone to watch the girls after school.

"You look . . . fabulous?" Carrie guessed.

"I know!" Ashley beamed. She pushed her blond hair out of her face. "Watch this."

Ashley dropped her backpack next to Mary-Kate's and began practicing her modeling walk. She stuck one hand on her hip and strolled back and forth across the room.

"What's up?" Carrie asked. "Something tells me you aren't doing that just for the exercise."

Ashley rushed over and grabbed Carrie's arm.

"The Fashion Van is coming to our school!" she said excitely. "I've been waiting for this my whole life! Can you believe it? I'm going to be a model!"

"Really?" Carrie asked. "That's great, Ashley! Oh, maybe that's what Jennifer wanted to talk to you about. She just called. She said to call her back right away—it's important."

I just saw her half an hour ago, Ashley thought. *What could she want to talk about?*

She grabbed a slice of apple from a plate on the dining table and took a bite. Then she hurried over to the phone.

While Ashley dialed Jennifer's number, Mary-Kate sat down at the table with Carrie. She opened her school notebook and began writing.

That's weird, Ashley thought. Why was Mary-Kate doing homework the minute they got home from school? She never touched her notebooks until she absolutely had to.

The phone rang three times. Finally Jennifer answered.

"Jennifer? You called?" Ashley asked, munching the apple as she talked.

"I've got some important news," Jennifer said. "First, I called the Horizon School of Modeling. They have an introductory session tomorrow after school—and there's still room in the class. I signed us up!"

"Cool," Ashley murmured.

"And then," Jennifer went on, lowering her voice, "you won't believe what I heard on the bus on the way home."

"What?" Ashley asked, taking another bite of apple.

"Your sister likes a boy!" Jennifer announced. "She's got a thing for Jeremy Ryan!"

Ashley's eyes popped wide open.

"No!" she cried, almost spitting out the apple. "How do you know? Who told you?"

"Angela saw Mary-Kate staring at him in class,"

Jennifer explained. "And when Miss Tabor called on Mary-Kate to answer a question, she didn't even hear her name being called! She couldn't take her eyes off the back of Jeremy's head."

"So? That doesn't mean she has a crush on him," Ashley argued.

"Oh, yes it does!" Jennifer insisted. "Because right after class Angela asked Mary-Kate if she liked him—and she admitted it!"

"No!" Ashley cried. She stared across the room, first at Carrie and then at Mary-Kate.

"Yes," Jennifer shot back. "She told Angela she'd give up her Michael Jordan autograph just to sit next to Jeremy!"

"Get out!" Ashley screeched into the phone.

"Whoa!" Carrie glanced at Mary-Kate. "Two 'no's' and a 'get out.' Sounds serious!"

"Oh, major!" Mary-Kate agreed. "One of Ashley's friends probably overplucked her eyebrows."

"I'll call you back," Ashley told Jennifer. Then she hung up the phone.

This is unbelievable! Ashley thought. *So much is happening at once. My very own twin sister likes a guy. And I'm finally going to get to model!*

This is going to be the most exciting week of my life!

6

CHAPTER TWO

"I've got great news," Ashley called out to Mary-Kate and Carrie. "Jennifer and I are going to take modeling lessons—at the Horizon School of Modeling!"

"You mean that place that's advertised on TV?" Mary-Kate asked. "I can't believe you'd fall for that hokey commercial."

"It could be my ticket to the big time," Ashley said. "And if you're really lucky, you can come, too."

She marched over to Mary-Kate and put her hands on her hips. "By the way, Mary-Kate," Ashley began, "Jennifer just told me that you like Jeremy Ryan. Is that true?"

Mary-Kate gasped.

"No way!" she insisted. She shook her head.

Ashley glanced at the notebook in front of Mary-Kate. The name Jeremy was written five times across the bottom of the page.

"Oh, yeah?" Ashley argued. "Then how come Jeremy's name is written in your notebook—inside an apple?"

Mary-Kate frowned at the page. "That's a heart—not an apple!" she snapped.

"Aha!" Ashley said, pointing at her sister. "I knew it! So, let me get this straight—you like a guy, and you didn't even tell me?"

Mary-Kate's face turned pink. She shrugged her shoulders. "I didn't want to say anything until I was really sure I liked him," she said.

"But you told Angela," Ashley pointed out.

"She forced it out of me," Mary-Kate admitted. "She said that otherwise she'd tell Jennifer."

"But she *did* tell Jennifer," Ashley said.

"You can't trust anyone these days." Mary-Kate sighed.

"So, go ahead, tell us." Carrie smiled. "Who's Jeremy?"

"He's just a new kid at school," Mary-Kate mumbled. "It's nothing."

"Nothing?" Carrie asked. "Come on—there's *got* to be more to this story. How did you meet him? What's he like? Does he even know you're alive?"

"We want details," Ashley insisted. "Because if you don't tell us, Angela will!"

"Okay, okay. He's in my science class," Mary-Kate said. "I noticed him because he has such . . . such incredible hair. And he's really nice when you talk to him. The first day he came to class, Miss Tabor made me explain stuff to him. Then he told me he was joining the wrestling team. It was . . . I don't know. Fun."

"You're in love!" Ashley cried.

"No!" Mary-Kate shouted. Then she lowered her voice. "I mean, I'm not even sure I really like him."

"Well, do you think about him a lot?" Carrie asked.

Mary-Kate gave Ashley a sheepish grin. "Is all the time a lot?"

"Wow, Mary-Kate!" Ashley cried. "You *are* in love!"

Ashley reached out quickly to hug her sister. This was the best! Finally she and Mary-Kate would have something to work on *together*. Because if there was one thing Ashley knew a lot about, it was having a crush on a boy.

"I *knew* this day would come!" Ashley gushed.

"Get a grip," Mary-Kate said, rolling her eyes. "For all I know, he's got a girlfriend."

"Don't worry about a thing," Ashley promised. "I'll make a few calls and find out. And I'll see if he's going to the dance on Friday. This is so exciting!"

Ashley grabbed the cordless phone and hurried to her room. She needed some privacy. She had to get the real story on Jeremy Ryan.

What if he does have a girlfriend already? Ashley worried. *It would be terrible for Mary-Kate to wind up with a broken heart on her first crush!*

Ashley flopped down on her bed and called Jennifer. But Jennifer wasn't home. Her mother said she'd gone out to the library to find some books on modeling. So Ashley called three more friends, until she finally reached someone.

"Listen, Michelle," Ashley said into the phone. "What do you know about Jeremy Ryan?"

"Um—that he's a hunk?" Michelle answered.

"Of course he's a hunk!" Ashley said impatiently. "That's not what I meant. Does he like anybody? Does he have a girlfriend?"

"I don't think so," Michelle said. "I heard him telling Jake Stone just two days ago that he hadn't decided whether he should go to the dance, since he didn't have anyone to go with."

"Excellent!" Ashley squealed.

"Why do you want to know?" Michelle asked. "Do you like him?"

"No," Ashley answered. "I don't even know him. It's Mary-Kate. She's got a huge crush on him. But don't say anything to Jeremy, okay?"

"No problem," Michelle promised.

"Thanks," Ashley said. "I'll talk to you tomorrow."

Then she hung up.

"Mary-Kate?" Ashley called as she dashed down the stairs. "Good news! He's . . ."

But the minute she hit the living room, Ashley put on the brakes. Her dad was there, talking to Mary-Kate. And if there was one thing Ashley and Mary-Kate agreed about, it was that they didn't want to tell their dad everything about boyfriend stuff.

"Hi, Ashley," Kevin Burke said, smiling at his daughter.

"Hi, Dad." Ashley crossed the room to Mary-Kate. "I have good news for you," she whispered. "Tell you later."

"News?" Kevin asked. "What news?"

Ashley tried to come up with something to say.

"Um, news?" Ashley said. "Oh, have you heard about the Fashion Van, Dad? It is *so* exciting. *Real Teen* magazine is sending photographers to school to pick some models for their 'Model of the Month' layout. And I want to try out!"

"Modeling at school? I don't know about that," Kevin said, shaking his head. "I think you girls should stay focused on your schoolwork."

Ashley hurried to her backpack and took out the permission slip.

"Come on, Dad!" she pleaded. "All you have to do is sign my permission slip and I get to do the layout!"

Kevin glanced at her sideways. "But, Ashley, don't the magazine people have to choose you first?"

"Of course they'll choose me!" Ashley said. "I was born to model. Watch."

She tossed her hair to one side, put a hand on her hip, and marched across the living room.

"Did you see that stuck-up look on my face?" Ashley asked proudly. "They can't teach that. You either have it—or you don't."

"I'm impressed," Kevin said with a laugh.

"So will you sign my permission slip?" Ashley

asked, shoving it toward her dad.

"And will you sign mine?" Mary-Kate chimed in, handing him another piece of paper.

"Huh?" Ashley's mouth fell open. "*You* want to try out for the fashion shoot?"

Kevin looked surprised, too. "Who are you?" he asked Mary-Kate. "And what have you done with my daughter, Mary-Kate?"

"Why shouldn't I model?" Mary-Kate asked, shrugging. "You get out of class for the interview. And you get a whole day off if they choose you."

"Ah," Kevin said, nodding. "*There's* my Mary-Kate!"

Ashley shook her head. "You can't just try out for this fashion shoot for a laugh," she pointed out. "It isn't about getting out of class. It's a career opportunity! It's my dream—my chance to model in New York City and get out of this little town!"

Mary-Kate rolled her eyes. "Hel-*lo!*" she said. "Little town? Are you kidding? This is Chicago!"

"So what?" Ashley said. "That's not the point. The point is, I really care about modeling—and you don't!"

"Look," Kevin said, pocketing the permission slips. "I'll check with the school about this fashion thing. And if it seems okay, I'll sign *both* of your slips."

"Thanks, Dad." Mary-Kate beamed.

"Oh, and by the way," Ashley said. "Jennifer and I want to sign up for this great modeling course. At the Horizon School of Modeling."

Kevin made a face. "Isn't that the place that's advertised on TV? It looks like a rip-off to me."

"It's not," Ashley insisted. "They teach you about hair and makeup and all kinds of cool stuff. Please," she begged. "The special introductory session is tomorrow afternoon. And it's half-price. Only ten dollars."

"Okay, okay," Kevin said. "Carrie can pick you up after school and take you there."

Carrie poked her head out of the kitchen. "I've always been curious about that ad myself," she said. "This will give me a chance to check it out."

"It'll be great," Ashley promised. "You'll see."

"By the way, Carrie," Kevin said, "I've got to go out for a while. I've got a meeting at the girls' school. They need another chaperone for the dance."

"No!" Ashley and Mary-Kate both cried at once.

"Why not?" Kevin asked. "You guys used to love it when I came to school stuff. Remember when I was Cowboy Kev at the school fair?"

"Dad, we *didn't* love it," Mary-Kate explained. "We weren't laughing *with* you. We were laughing *at* you."

"Oh," Kevin said. "Oh, well. I already promised I'd be there for the dance. So you're stuck with me."

"Okay, Dad," Mary-Kate said as Kevin went into the kitchen. "As long as you don't dance!"

She turned to Ashley. "So—what's the scoop on Jeremy?" she asked.

"He doesn't have a girlfriend. He's absolutely available!" Ashley exclaimed. "I say we find out if he's going to the dance."

Mary-Kate got a dreamy look on her face. "Going to the dance," she mused. "With Jeremy." She practically floated up the stairs.

I don't believe it, Ashley thought, gazing after her sister. *First Mary-Kate gets a crush on a boy—and now she wants to dance with him. Suddenly she's acting so . . . so different.*

But the weirdest thing was that Mary-Kate was actually going to enter the modeling contest. *It's too bad she doesn't have a chance of winning. She doesn't know the first thing about modeling,* Ashley thought.

I'd better help Mary-Kate with Jeremy. That way she won't be too upset when she doesn't get to model.

And that way we'll both get what we want!

CHAPTER THREE

"There he is!" Mary-Kate whispered to her sister. The two of them stood outside the boys' locker room, near the gym.

Jeremy Ryan, a tall, cute guy with thick, sandy-brown hair, was dressed for wrestling practice. He put one foot up against a wall and stretched his leg muscles.

Mary-Kate felt her heart sink. *How can I just go up and talk to him?* she thought.

"Okay, just be calm," Ashley coached. "Do you remember what I told you to say?"

"No! I don't," Mary-Kate moaned. "I'm so nervous, I don't remember my own name! And besides, I don't think we're supposed to hang out this close to the boys' locker room."

"Oh, this is fine," Ashley reassured her. "You just can't go *inside*. I found out that was a no-no."

Inside the boys' locker room? Mary-Kate rolled her eyes. Was there anything her sister *wouldn't* do to get near a boy?

"Okay, here he comes," Ashley whispered.

"Help!" Mary-Kate moaned. "What am I supposed to say? Something about the dance?"

"Never mind," Ashley said. "I'll handle this."

Jeremy started past the two girls as if he didn't even see them. But as soon as he was in front of Mary-Kate, Ashley bumped into her sister's arm. All of Mary-Kate's books tumbled to the floor.

"Ooops. Sorry," Ashley said.

Oh, man, Mary-Kate thought. *Now what am I supposed to do?*

Jeremy bent down quickly and picked up her books.

Say thank you, Mary-Kate told herself. *Say something!*

But her throat had a huge lump in it. She couldn't think of a *thing* to say.

"Thanks," Ashley said, watching Jeremy. "I'm Ashley. This is my sister, Mary-Kate."

"Hi," Jeremy said. He stared at Mary-Kate hard,

then looked at Ashley. Then back at Mary-Kate. "Hey—you're in my science class."

Mary-Kate just nodded. *This is amazing! He can tell us apart. He knows it's me in his class—not Ashley.*

As he handed her the books, Mary-Kate felt her face getting hot.

He's soooo cute! she thought. *I love the way his hair waves and dips on the sides. He looks awesome in those wrestling clothes.*

Mary-Kate felt her sister nudging her.

Oh, yeah, Mary-Kate thought. *I'm supposed to ask him if he's going to the dance. Right.*

The only problem was, she couldn't form the words in her mouth.

"Uh," she stammered, "did you, I mean, uh, are you going to, uh . . . finish that science homework?"

"What science homework?" Jeremy asked, looking confused.

Uh-oh, Mary-Kate thought. *We didn't have science homework last night. Whoops!*

She felt Ashley nudge her again. "The dance," Ashley whispered. "Ask about the dance!"

Mary-Kate took a deep breath.

"What I mean is, uh, on Friday?" Mary-Kate babbled. "Are you going? To the dance?"

I sound like a complete idiot! she realized. She wished with all her heart that she could just disappear into the floor.

Mary-Kate shot Ashley a pleading glance. *Help me out here!* she thought.

Ashley jumped right into the conversation. "Mary-Kate brings up a good point, Jeremy," she said quickly. "Are you going to the dance on Friday?"

"Yeah, I'll be there," he answered. Then he turned and started to walk toward the gym.

"Well, you know, Jeremy," Ashley called, running after him. "Mary-Kate's going Friday night, too. Maybe you two could dance together."

"Well," Jeremy hesitated. "Uh, sure. But, I, uh, only swing dance."

Swing dance? That's so cool! Mary-Kate thought. *Too bad I don't know how.*

"Swing dance?" Ashley repeated, gulping.

"Yeah," Jeremy said. "I don't even bother with anything else now." He gave a little shrug.

Mary-Kate swallowed hard. *Well, that's that,* she thought.

"What an amazing coincidence!" Ashley said. She beamed. "Mary-Kate is a fabulous swing dancer!"

Mary-Kate's eyes flew wide open. "I am?" she blurted out.

"Don't be so modest," Ashley insisted. "You should see her room, Jeremy. It's full of dance trophies. You two will definitely have to hook up."

Ashley! Mary-Kate tried to beam her sister a mental command to shut up.

"Yeah," Jeremy said. He glanced over toward the wrestling team. "Uh, that sounds okay."

Just then the coach blew a whistle.

"Well, I've got to go," Jeremy said, dashing off.

"See you Friday!" Ashley called after him.

"Yeah. Friday," he mumbled back.

Mary-Kate watched him join the other guys on the team. Then she whirled around and faced her twin.

"Are you crazy?" she snapped. "I can't swing dance! Now what am I going to do?"

"Hey, I'm just the matchmaker," Ashley said with a shrug. "It's up to you to make the relationship work."

Then she had the nerve to walk away!

"Thanks a lot!" Mary-Kate called after her. "You talked me into this mess. How am I supposed to get myself out?"

Maybe she could break a leg. Or take an

unexpected trip to Mexico. Or come down with a terrible illness.

No. There was only one answer. And Mary-Kate knew what it was.

She *had* to learn how to swing dance by Friday. Period.

But what if I can't? Mary-Kate thought. *What if I just can't do it?*

CHAPTER FOUR

"Last chance!" Ashley said to Mary-Kate after school that day. "Are you sure you don't want to come with us?"

Ashley and Jennifer stood on the sidewalk near the front entrance.

"To that rip-off modeling school?" Mary-Kate answered. "You've got to be kidding. I wouldn't spend ten cents on those lessons—let alone ten dollars!"

"It's not a rip-off," Ashley insisted. She and Jennifer began to walk down the block. "It's the best way to learn all about the fashion world."

"No, thanks," Mary-Kate called after them. "I've got basketball practice. I've got to learn how to improve my jump shot. I don't have *time* to learn how to model!"

Ashley and Jennifer hurried to the parking lot. Carrie was waiting in her car.

"Carrie, do you think Mary-Kate's right?" Jennifer asked after she and Ashley hopped into the back seat. "I mean, about the Horizon School of Modeling. Mary-Kate says it's a rip-off."

"No way," Ashley interrupted before Carrie could answer. "I watched the commercial five times. It says: 'After just one lesson, you'll have enough poise, grace, and style to walk down a runway in your pajamas!'"

"Not in my pajamas," Jennifer said. "They have holes in them!"

Ashley laughed and flipped her hair over her shoulders. "Forget the pajamas. The main thing is that it's perfect training for the Fashion Van tryouts. So don't worry. It's going to be really great."

"So Carrie, what do *you* think?" Jennifer asked again.

"There's just one way to find out," Carrie replied. "Try it and see if you like it."

Ten minutes later they drove up in front of the modeling school.

"You go ahead in," Carrie said. "I'm going to

park the car. I'll meet you in the lobby after the class."

Ashley and Jennifer walked into the building and were led into a large room filled with folding chairs. A model's runway was set up down the middle of the room. The chairs faced the runway on both sides.

Lots of other girls were already there, so most of the seats were filled.

"Looks like we have to sit in the back," Jennifer complained.

Ashley's heart sank. Jennifer was right—the room was full. They wouldn't be able to see very well from the back row.

"Oh, well, come on," Ashley urged. "They're starting."

"Hello, girls." An older woman with blond hair pulled back into a chic bun came out onto the runway and spoke into a microphone. "I'm Liz Horizon, the owner of the Horizon School of Modeling. I am so glad to have you all with me today."

Liz Horizon spread her arms out, gesturing to the crowd of girls.

"Our next generation of supermodels!" she announced proudly.

"This is so cool!" Jennifer whispered to Ashley.

"I know!" Ashley agreed.

"Now, before we get started, we have a short video I'd like you to watch," Liz said.

Ashley glanced at Jennifer.

"A video?" Jennifer whispered. "We paid ten dollars to watch a video?"

Ashley shrugged and turned toward the screen. A moment later the video came on. It was just like the commercial Ashley had seen on TV—only longer. Much longer. It showed girls Ashley's age walking up and down a runway. But it didn't teach anything about how to be a model.

Finally it was over.

"Now, girls," Liz Horizon said, "we have so many of you here today, we won't have the chance to work with everyone. But we'll try to get a few of you up here, onto the runway. Do I have volunteers?"

Instantly Ashley's arm shot into the air.

"Me!" Ashley pleaded, sitting up as straight and tall as she could. She and Jennifer waved their arms wildly. "Pick me!"

Liz Horizon chose the first three girls in the front row.

Everyone else in the room moaned.

"Now, girls, if you sign up for our eight-week course, you'll *all* get a chance," Liz told them. "Today I can only use three of you. Whoops! I made a mistake. I need four girls."

Her eyes scanned the room and quickly landed on Ashley. "You," Liz said, pointing toward the back row. "Come up front."

Yes! Ashley thought.

She hurried to the edge of the modeling runway, her heart pounding with excitement.

"Where do you want me?" Ashley asked.

"Over there," Liz said. She pointed to a folding chair beside the runway. Next to it was a small table with a boom box on top. "You're running the tape recorder," Liz explained. "When the girls are on the runway, turn on the music. When I signal you, turn it off."

Ashley's jaw dropped. "I'm just the deejay?" she asked.

Liz nodded. "And pull your chair more off to the side, so you won't be in the way," she added.

This stinks! Ashley thought as she plopped down by the tape recorder. *But at least from here, I can see the runway better.*

For the next twenty minutes, Ashley punched the Play and Stop buttons over and over. The three girls from the front row paraded up and down the runway. They looked really expert—as if they'd done it a million times before.

I bet those girls have already taken the modeling course, Ashley thought. *They were picked just so the school would look good.*

"Stick your hip out a little more, Sara," Liz called from the floor. "And don't smile. Smiling is out in the fashion business."

I'll have to remember that, Ashley thought. *Don't smile.*

Ashley pushed her lower lip out in a pout. She practiced making her face look totally grumpy.

Ten minutes later, the demonstration was over. "You may return to your seats now, girls," Liz said.

Ashley hurried back to sit beside Jennifer.

"I'm afraid we're out of time for today," Liz told the audience. "But we have special free gifts for you. My assistant is passing them out."

Ashley's eyes lit up. She craned her neck to see what the free gift was. It looked like a plastic bag with free samples of makeup in it.

"Cool!" Jennifer whispered.

"Now, remember," Liz Horizon said. "You can't become a model just by practicing at home. There are special things you need to learn to look like a professional model. For instance, you need to use a lot of makeup. But it has to be applied just right on girls your age. That's what we're here to teach you—and that's what the fashion magazines want." Ashley watched Liz's assistant passing out the free gifts. She only had four of them left. And she was still two rows in front of Ashley and Jennifer.

"Unfortunately, it looks as if we don't have enough free gifts to go around," Liz announced. "If you don't get one, stop at the front desk. We'll give you a coupon worth five dollars off the price of the eight-week course. And thank you all again for coming."

Ashley and Jennifer filed out of the room with the other girls.

"Oh, man," Jennifer said when they reached the hallway. "We didn't even get the gift. This was a total waste of time."

"No, it wasn't." Ashley laughed. "At least we know we need to use a lot of makeup tomorrow."

"I was going to do that anyway," Jennifer pointed out.

"Me too," Ashley said. "But the most important thing we learned was: Don't smile. No matter what we do, we *won't* smile at the tryouts tomorrow. Got that?"

"Don't worry," Jennifer said. "I wouldn't dream

of smiling at the camera. What do you think I am— an amateur?"

Right, Ashley thought. *We already knew all of that stuff. Jennifer and I are cut out to be supermodels!*

Now all we have to do is choose an outfit, show up at school, and the job is ours!

CHAPTER FIVE

"Let's go, Ashley," Kevin called up the stairs the next morning. "We're going to be late!"

"Forget it, Dad," Mary-Kate said. "Today is model interview day for the Fashion Van. She'll *never* be ready!"

"I'm ready now," Ashley announced as she paraded down the stairs.

And wait till they see how fabulous I look! she thought.

Ashley pouted in that special way she had learned in modeling school. She walked especially slowly, so Mary-Kate and her dad could check out her outfit. It was a light blue slip-dress with beading at the top and high platform shoes to match. Her hair was exactly the way she liked it best—piled up on her head, with lots of pieces twisted into crazy loops.

"Good morning, Ashley," Kevin said to her. "Will you be eating in the *formal* cafeteria today?"

Ashley ignored him. She glanced at her sister to see what she was wearing.

Oh, no, Ashley thought. *Not those black velvet overalls and a ribbed T-shirt! The Fashion Van people won't even notice her in that.*

Ashley thought about helping Mary-Kate. *If I lend her an outfit, at least she won't embarrass herself in front of all those fashion people!*

But there wasn't enough time. Kevin was already out the door.

"I thought the magazine said they wanted kids who look natural." Mary-Kate stared at Ashley's outfit.

"Oh, please." Ashley sighed. "They *have* to say that. It's the law or something. But they pick the kids they notice. And this outfit just screams, 'Look at me.'"

"Really?" Mary-Kate cracked. "Because I'm hearing, 'Look at me—I'm a freak.'"

Don't pay any attention, Ashley told herself. *What does she know about modeling, anyway?*

"That's enough," Kevin called from the doorway. "Let's go or we'll be late."

By the time they got to school, Ashley was so excited she was ready to explode.

"Look! The Fashion Van is parked outside!" she cried as she dashed from the car. Mary-Kate followed her into the school building.

Jennifer was waiting for Ashley by her locker. She was dressed in a slinky black dress, three rhinestone necklaces, and stacked heels.

"They're holding the tryouts first thing this morning!" Jennifer squealed.

"Cool!" Ashley answered, grabbing her friend's hand.

"I got our passes from Mr. Morrow, so we don't even have to go to class," Jennifer explained. "We're in the first group."

"That's great—thanks," Ashley said. "I am *so* ready for this."

Jennifer squinted, checking out Ashley's hair and makeup. "Hmmm," Jennifer said. "You could use a little more lipliner."

"Oh, no," Ashley cried. "Do you think so? I've got to fix it—quick!"

Frantically she dashed into the girls' rest room and pulled a pencil out of her bag.

A moment later her friend Michelle walked in wearing jeans and a turtleneck top. "Wow," Michelle said, glancing at Ashley's dress. "Is the dance tonight? I thought it wasn't until Friday."

"Hel-*lo!* I'm dressed like this for the Fashion Van tryouts—or did you forget?" Ashley asked.

"Oh, no, I just tried out a few minutes ago," Michelle said. "They're looking for kids who look real—like the title of the magazine says. *Real Teen.* Remember?"

Yeah, right, Ashley thought. She sure wasn't going to fall for that "we want natural-looking kids" line!

"They told me I looked great," Michelle went on.

"That's nice," Ashley said politely.

Why make Michelle feel bad? she decided. *They probably tell everyone that they're great. Some people are cut out for this modeling thing—and some aren't!*

Ashley hurried back to the hall and found Jennifer. Then the two of them hurried to the west-wing hallway, where the Fashion Van tryouts were being held.

A famous model named Tara James was there with the photographers. She told each girl where to go and what to do.

"Just stand near that locker and pretend you're

getting your books," Tara told Jennifer. "Then turn around when we tell you to and smile."

Smile? Ashley thought. *No way. They must mean they want a pouty smile. Or a snooty smile, or something.*

Jennifer turned the corners of her lips up in a little smirk.

"That's great!" the photographer said as Jennifer posed.

Pretty soon, it was Ashley's turn. The photographer used a camcorder to videotape her tryout. Ashley gave them her most stuck-up pout for about half of the poses. For the other half, she arched her back, tossed her head, and tried to look really glamorous.

"That was great!" the photographer said. "Thanks. We'll put the results on the bulletin board by the end of school today. Good luck."

Okay, Ashley thought. *I can wait until the end of the day. But just barely!*

She started to walk away, back toward her homeroom class. But just then, Mary-Kate showed up.

"Hold on," Ashley whispered to Jennifer. "I want to watch Mary-Kate try out."

"What for?" Jennifer asked. "She doesn't have a chance."

"She *is* my twin, you know!" Ashley said, sticking up for her sister.

"Please," Jennifer moaned. "There's no comparison. *You* know how to dress. How to walk. How to . . . everything! She knows how to shoot a what-do-you-call-it shot on the basketball court."

"A layup shot," Ashley said.

She watched for a minute as Mary-Kate posed for the photographers. Mary-Kate gave them a sweet smile each time they asked for it. But she didn't strut or twirl or anything.

Come on, Mary-Kate, Ashley coached her silently. *Lift your chin! Swing your hips!*

She waved her hands to try to get Mary-Kate's attention.

But Mary-Kate ignored her.

Oh well, I tried, Ashley thought. "Come on," she said to Jennifer. "Let's go back to class."

But Jennifer wasn't quite ready to leave.

She marched up to Tara. "I just want to tell you it's been a pleasure working with you," Jennifer gushed. "And I'm looking forward to doing a really spectacular shoot."

"I hope you had a good time at the tryouts," Tara replied.

"Thank you," Jennifer called.

"Laying it on a little thick, aren't you?" Ashley asked, rolling her eyes.

"I just wanted to let her know that when she picks me, she'll be working with a professional," Jennifer explained as she headed down the hall toward their homeroom. "Now all we have to do is wait!"

Right, Ashley thought. *Wait. All the way until three o'clock. How can I stand it? Today is going to be the longest day of my life!*

CHAPTER SIX

"This is it!" Ashley declared as she and Mary-Kate hurried from their sixth period class. "The start of my lifetime career as a model. But don't worry. I won't forget the little people—the ones I knew on my way to the top."

She patted Mary-Kate on the head when she said "little people." Then she laughed, because it was true. Even though they were twins, Ashley was just a bit taller than her sister. And she looked a lot taller today, since she was wearing platform shoes and Mary-Kate wasn't.

"Give me a break," Mary-Kate complained. "On your way to the top of *what?*"

"The modeling world, of course," Ashley replied.

"Come on—let's go see the list. I hope they spelled my name right!"

Ashley pushed her way through the crowded school hallway toward the main bulletin board. That's where the Fashion Van would post the list of kids who were chosen for the photo shoot.

But when she got to the hall, she couldn't get close enough to the board to read the piece of paper. The hallway was packed with kids clamoring to see who was going to be in the magazine fashion layout.

Wow, Ashley thought, glancing around. *Even kids who didn't try out are hanging out here!*

Then she smiled to herself.

They probably just want to be around us, she decided. *So they can tell their friends, "I knew Ashley Burke when . . ."*

Her friends Max and Brian were hovering at the back of the mob, watching the crowd at the board. Ashley stood near them, waiting for her turn to read the notice.

"A lot of these girls are going to be disappointed," Max said to Brian.

"Yeah, and they're going to need a strong shoulder to cry on," Brian agreed. "And I've got two of them!"

Ashley couldn't imagine ever crying on Brian's shoulders.

"There's Jennifer," Mary-Kate said, giving Ashley a nudge and pointing toward the front of the crowd. "Hey, Jennifer. Did they pick you?" Mary-Kate called.

"For that stupid photo layout?" Jennifer said angrily. "Who cares?"

"Whoa," Mary-Kate murmured to Ashley. "Sounds like she tanked."

Well, I'm not surprised, Ashley thought, trying to stay calm. *They can't choose too many girls who are totally beautiful and have attitude—like me. And like Jennifer. They probably didn't want us all to look alike!*

Still, Ashley started to feel a little bit nervous and jumpy in her stomach.

Jennifer is supercool, she thought. *And her fashion sense is perfect. If she doesn't get picked . . . will I?*

Ashley pushed a little harder, trying to wedge her way through the crowd to the bulletin board. One by one the kids at the front read the list and then turned away.

Finally it was Ashley's turn.

"Well?" Mary-Kate called from off to the side. "Did you make it, Ashley?"

Ashley's mouth dropped open. She couldn't

believe what she was seeing. There it was—in big black letters.

Mary-Kate Burke.

Her *twin sister's* name was on the list—but hers wasn't!

"Did you make it?" Mary-Kate called again, a little louder this time.

"No," Ashley said, pushing her way out of the crowd. "But *you* did."

CHAPTER SEVEN

"Guess what? I'm going to be a model!" Mary-Kate announced to Carrie as the twins burst into the house later that afternoon.

"You are? That's great!" Carrie answered.

"I can't believe it. I'm a model! I'm a model!" Mary-Kate repeated as she climbed the stairs to her room.

Don't rub it in, Ashley thought, watching her disappear.

I'm a model.

Those are the words I should be saying! Ashley thought. Instantly she felt her eyes fill with tears.

"Uh-oh," Carrie said, glancing at the expression on Ashley's face. "Looks to me like you're having a

41

little problem with this, aren't you?"

"It's just not fair," Ashley burst out. "I mean, Mary-Kate doesn't care a thing about clothes. She doesn't even like shopping! How could they pick her, and not me?"

Carrie passed Ashley a plate of freshly baked oatmeal raisin cookies and gave her a pat on the arm.

"I don't know, honey," Carrie said. "It's hard to figure things like this out sometimes. I know how much the modeling job meant to you. But sometimes life just isn't fair, you know?"

I do know, Ashley thought. But that didn't make it any easier to accept.

"Maybe the Fashion Van will come again next year," Carrie said. "You'll have another chance at it someday, I'm sure."

"Next year?" Ashley said. "I don't have that long. I'm not going to be young forever!" She grabbed another cookie and marched upstairs to her room.

Carrie's right, she thought. *I can't give up. But I can't wait, either. I've got to become a model now!*

Mary-Kate was lying on her bed reading a magazine.

"Mary-Kate?" Ashley began, plunging right in.

"We need to talk. About this whole modeling thing."

Mary-Kate jumped and stuffed the magazine under a pillow. But not before Ashley caught a glimpse of the cover. It was *Real Teen!*

Wow, Ashley thought. *She's never read* Real Teen *before. What's going on? Is Mary-Kate really taking this modeling thing seriously? Or is she just reading the magazine to find out what modeling is all about?*

Either way, it doesn't matter, Ashley decided. *It still isn't fair for Mary-Kate to do the layout.*

"Talk? About what?" Mary-Kate asked.

"It's simple," Ashley explained. "This should be *my* fashion shoot—and you know it. You only tried out so you could miss class. *I* tried out because fashion is my *life.*"

"How do you know why I tried out?" Mary-Kate argued.

"Well, you said so. Besides, what other reason could there be?" Ashley said. "You don't care about clothes. Everyone knows that."

Mary-Kate shrugged. "Well, it's too late to do anything about it now," she said. "They picked me, and that's that."

"That's where you're wrong," Ashley said, sitting down next to her sister. She handed Mary-Kate an oatmeal cookie. "I could pretend to be you. We look so much alike, no one would ever know the difference."

"Forget it, Ashley," Mary-Kate said. "Every time we switch places, we get into trouble. I won't do it."

Ashley thought fast. There had to be a way!

"There's another possibility," Ashley said slowly. "If you injured yourself, they'd have to use some-one else for the photo shoot. And since I look exactly like you—they'd pick me! Right?"

Mary-Kate dropped the cookie on the bed. "You want me to *hurt* myself?" she gasped, her eyes opening wide.

Ashley shook her head. "I'm not talking broken bones," she said quickly. "Maybe just a sprained ankle?"

"You're nuts! I'm not going to sprain my ankle for you!" Mary-Kate cried.

"I don't mean *really* sprain it. Just *pretend* to be hurt. Please, Mary-Kate," Ashley begged. "I need to do this. I want it so badly. It's my once-in-a-lifetime chance."

Mary-Kate stared at Ashley for a moment. "This is really important to you, isn't it?" she asked.

Yes! Ashley thought. *More than you know!*

"It's my dream," she said.

Mary-Kate let out a sigh. "Well," she said finally. "I guess I *could* fake a head cold—on *one* condition."

"Oh, thank you! Thank you!" Ashley cried, grabbing her sister and hugging her. "I'll do anything you want. What is it?"

"You've got to teach me to swing dance by Friday," Mary-Kate answered. "So I can dance with Jeremy!"

Teach her to swing dance by Friday? Ashley thought. *How am I supposed to do that? I can't swing dance myself. I don't have a clue!*

Oh, well. I'll figure something out, she decided quickly.

"You've got it!" Ashley promised. "No problem. You'll be tearing up the dance floor by Friday night. Oh, thank you, Mary-Kate! Thank you!"

Ashley leaped off Mary-Kate's bed and headed for the door.

"Where are you going?" Mary-Kate asked. "If you're going to teach me to swing dance, we'd better get started."

"We can do that later," Ashley said quickly. "First I've got to go call Jennifer. She's going to *hate* me!"

"Oh, wow!" she added. "I'm going to be a model!"

CHAPTER EIGHT

Mary-Kate sat glumly on her bed as Ashley raced out of the room.

"I'm going to be a model!" Ashley called all the way down the stairs.

"Fine. Go on and celebrate," Mary-Kate mumbled, even though Ashley was too far away to hear. Then she flopped down on her back and stared up at the ceiling.

She realized she was disappointed that she wouldn't be going on the fashion shoot.

But why? She'd never cared about modeling before. Modeling was Ashley's thing, not hers.

Maybe it was because she had started liking Jeremy Ryan. And if she did the photo shoot at school, everyone would notice her—including Jeremy!

Mary-Kate rolled onto her stomach, feeling grumpy.

Okay, it's true, she thought. *I didn't used to be so interested in clothes, or boys, or makeup.*

But maybe I've changed. Maybe I do care about clothes—now that I'm trying to get a guy to notice me.

Sure, I know how important modeling is to Ashley. And I told her she could go on the fashion shoot. So I'll just forget about it.

But that doesn't mean I have to forget about clothes, too.

Mary-Kate jumped up and hurried to her closet to stare at her clothes. A blue sweater set and black pants were hanging near the front. She remembered that Ashley had complimented her on that outfit the day she bought it.

Okay, Mary-Kate decided, pulling the outfit from the closet. *This is what I'll wear tomorrow.*

Tomorrow was going to be a special day. Miss Tabor was going to divide the science class into study groups.

And with any luck, Mary-Kate would be in Jeremy's group.

I want to look especially nice, Mary-Kate thought.

Otherwise, Jeremy might change his mind about Friday—and about dancing with me!

"Class! Class, settle down!" Miss Tabor called the next afternoon. "If you can't work together in groups, you'll have to go back to your desks and work by yourselves."

Mary-Kate grinned at Jeremy, who was sitting across from her at a large round table.

He rolled his eyes at the teacher. Then he leaned closer to Mary-Kate.

"So, what do you think we should do first?" he asked. He pointed to a picture of a cell in his science book. "Copy this diagram of the cell or memorize its parts?"

"I don't know," Mary-Kate said. "I think cells are real confusing. I mean, who can remember what mitochondria are anyhow?"

"But mitochondria are so cool," Jeremy said. "They look like alien spaceships flying around the cell."

Mary-Kate laughed. "Spaceships filled with little green mitochodrians," she joked.

"Yeah." Jeremy grinned at her. "See, Mary-Kate? Science is out of this world!"

Wow, Mary-Kate thought. *Jeremy is really funny.*

He's not only gorgeous—he's got a great sense of humor, too.

Marcie Lewis came back from the pencil sharpener. She slipped into her seat.

"Alien spaceships?" she asked. "What are you talking about? We're supposed to be studying biology, not talking about *Star Wars*."

Jeremy laughed. "But I love *Star Wars*," he protested.

"*Star Wars?* Me too!" Mary-Kate blurted out.

We have so much in common! she thought, feeling a glow inside. *I wonder if he realizes that?*

Mary-Kate tried to read the expression on Jeremy's face. He shot her another smile. But she wasn't sure what it meant.

Was it a sign that he actually liked her? Or was he just making fun of Marcie for butting in?

"So, Jeremy," Marcie said, "are you going to the dance Friday night?"

Jeremy was staring down at his book. He raised his eyes to glance at Mary-Kate.

"Uh, yeah," he said.

"Well, are you going to *dance*?" Marcie asked boldly. "Or are you just going to stand around and watch, like half the other guys?"

"I only swing dance," Jeremy said.

"Me too," Mary-Kate chimed in quickly. She flashed Jeremy a smile.

At least I hope I swing dance by Friday! Mary-Kate thought. *So far, I haven't learned a step!*

"Swing dancing is so cool!" Marcie gushed to Jeremy. She totally ignored Mary-Kate. "Maybe you can teach *me*."

Maybe you can just go away, Mary-Kate thought. She glanced at Jeremy. He didn't want to dance with Marcie, did he?

Jeremy looked uncomfortable. He gazed from Mary-Kate to Marcie and back.

"Nah," Jeremy said. "I don't think so. Most of the steps I know are so hard, you have to be an expert to do them."

Yikes! Mary-Kate thought. *An expert? That's what I'm supposed to be. Ashley told Jeremy I'm a swing-dancing champion.*

But if she didn't get started soon, she was going to look like a complete fool on Friday night.

And it would be all Ashley's fault!

CHAPTER NINE

"Ashley, I'm feeling amazingly healthy," Mary-Kate announced after school that day.

"Good for you," Ashley said with a shrug. "What's that supposed to mean?"

"It means the dance is in two days, and you still haven't taught me to swing dance," Mary-Kate warned. "And if I don't learn by Friday, I *won't* be getting a cold for the fashion shoot on Monday!"

"Whoa. Okay, okay." Ashley got the point. "Let's get to work. I'll find some music. You take off your shoes. It's easier if you take your shoes off, right?"

"Don't ask me!" Mary-Kate shot back. "You're supposed to be the expert! You *did* learn how to swing dance from Jennifer, didn't you?"

"Uh, yeah. Sure. Jennifer taught me everything," Ashley said.

Mary-Kate kicked off her shoes and pushed back the rug in their room. *I hope Ashley knows what she's talking about,* Mary-Kate thought.

"Okay," Ashley said, taking Mary-Kate's hand. "Let's see. I think there's something called a rock-step. It's kind of like this."

Mary-Kate just stood there and watched her sister. But Ashley wasn't exactly moving in time to the music. Her feet couldn't keep the beat at all.

"Now twist, twist, twist," Ashley called out, "and then twirl!"

With that, Ashley spun around, twisting Mary-Kate's arm around her back. But Ashley was too fast. Mary-Kate had to let go, and Ashley slid to the floor.

"Ow!" Ashley complained. "You didn't twirl, Mary-Kate!"

"How am I supposed to twirl when you're breaking my arm off?" Mary-Kate complained. "Tell the truth, Ashley. You don't know what you're doing—do you?"

"Not exactly," Ashley admitted. "But give me a chance! If I could just watch someone swing dancing—someone who's really good at it—I'm sure I'd have no trouble figuring it out."

"Did someone mention my name?" a voice said from the doorway of the girls' room.

Both girls' heads snapped around. Carrie was standing there, bouncing in time to the music. "If you want to learn how to swing dance," she said, "you've come to the right place."

"Carrie!" Ashley cried. "Really? You can swing dance? Because Mary-Kate *has* to learn how by Friday."

"No problem," Carrie replied. "I can have you both doing jumps and swing-splits in no time! But we need more space. Come on downstairs, and we'll push all the living room furniture back. Dance class is in session!"

"Yes!" Mary-Kate cheered. *Maybe this way I can swing dance with Jeremy before Marcie gets to him!*

She and Ashley hurried downstairs behind Carrie. They helped her push the couch and chairs to the wall. Finally they had a big, open space to dance in.

"All right!" Carrie announced, clapping her hands together. "Let's boogie!"

Patiently Carrie explained the terms and steps for swing dancing. She didn't even put the music on until Mary-Kate understood what a rock-step was.

And a twist. And a slide, twirl, slide.

Then she cranked up the music, and they practiced slowly at first, then faster. Within an hour Mary-Kate was starting to get it.

She danced with Ashley, who was trying to learn, too.

"Five, six, seven, eight," Carrie called out above the music. "Twist and twist and rock-step! Twist and spin and . . ."

Oops! Mary-Kate was supposed to spin, but she missed a step. An instant later she was all wrapped up in Ashley's arms.

"Form a human pretzel!" Carrie joked, laughing at the two of them.

"I'm never going to get this!" Mary-Kate said.

"You'll be fine," Carrie assured her. "Don't worry. I've got two more days to teach you the basics. Let's try it again. Five, six, seven, eight . . ."

Mary-Kate took Ashley's hand and tried to get back into the rhythm of it.

Basic step, rock-step. Basic step, rock-step.

"Now cuddle!" Carrie called out.

Mary-Kate leaned in for the cuddle move, but Ashley spun her out instead. Mary-Kate slid across the room, and landed half on the couch, half off.

"You're improving, Mary-Kate," Carrie said.

Mary-Kate could tell she was trying to sound encouraging.

"Yeah? Tell that to my sore feet!" Mary-Kate moaned.

Carrie switched off the music. "Maybe we need a rest," she suggested. "We'll try again after dinner, okay?"

The front door opened and their dad walked in. Kevin stared at the way the furniture was pushed around, then grinned.

"Hey," he said cheerfully to Carrie. "I hate what you've done with the room. It just screams, 'Put me back!'"

"Oh, hi, professor," Carrie said, laughing. "I was just teaching the girls how to swing dance for Friday night."

"Really?" Kevin's face lit up. "Maybe I should brush up on some of my moves. It's been a long time since I 'boogied down.'"

Instantly, he started disco dancing around the living room. He pointed his finger in the air and put a hand on his hip. Mary-Kate thought he looked totally weird.

"No!" Mary-Kate screamed. "Promise me that you won't even *think* about doing that on Friday night!"

Kevin stopped dancing. "Give me some credit, will you?" he laughed. "I was just kidding."

"So, you won't dance?" Ashley asked. She made it sound more like an order than a request.

"Not like that," Kevin agreed. "Now swing dancing—that's another story. That's something I'm really good at!"

"You are *not* wearing a name tag at this dance," Ashley announced to her father. "Got that? I don't want anyone to know you're my dad!"

"Okay, okay," Kevin said. "Don't worry. Friday night, I'll be the Invisible Man."

Maybe I'm the one who should be invisible, Mary-Kate thought. A worried feeling crept back into her stomach.

Friday night could be a total disaster!

CHAPTER TEN

"Is my hair all right?" Mary-Kate asked Ashley.

Mary-Kate stared into the mirror in her room and fluffed her hair. Ashley glanced up at Mary-Kate, then fiddled with a clip in her own hair.

"It's perfect, of course," Ashley replied. "It *has* to be—*I* did it for you!"

"I'm just so nervous about the dance tonight," Mary-Kate said. "What if Jeremy tries to swing me around his waist, and I go flying across the gym?"

"Don't worry," Ashley said. "You'll be fine. You've really picked up on those moves Carrie taught us. And if Jeremy tries to take it too fast, just tell him you twisted your ankle. You can say it was at a swing-dancing contest. And that you're supposed to go easy for a while."

"Twisted my ankle? That's the second time this week that you've suggested I hurt my ankle!" Mary-Kate complained.

"Hey—I'm just thinking of *you*," Ashley insisted. "Besides, what if you *did* have to use that excuse at the dance? Then you could say the same thing on Monday—to get out of the fashion shoot!"

Mary-Kate rolled her eyes and headed for the door.

"Come on," she said. "Let's go before I totally chicken out."

Mary-Kate checked herself in the mirror one more time. Yeah—her black turtleneck sweater looked pretty terrific with her red skirt and black tights.

Of course, Ashley looked fabulous, too. She was wearing a short black velvet dress printed with gray butterflies all over it. And a pearl-gray sweater to match.

Both girls had their hair piled up high, with loopy pieces clipped in lots of different directions.

After one last glance in the mirror, Mary-Kate headed downstairs. Ashley followed her. Carrie was sitting on the couch, waiting for them.

"Oh, look at you!" Carrie cried as the girls came

down the stairs. "All set for your dance. And you look so beautiful!"

She stood up to give each girl a hug.

Mary-Kate gulped. The closer she got to leaving the house, the more nervous she felt.

"Thanks. I just hope I get to dance with Jeremy before I throw up all over myself," Mary-Kate murmured.

"Maybe I'll drop in at the dance, just to see how much fun you're having," Carrie suggested.

"That's fine—if we ever *get* to the dance," Ashley complained. "It's getting late. Where's Dad?"

"Right here!" Kevin announced, bursting into the living room with a camera in his hands.

Quickly he snapped a picture, before the girls could complain.

"Oh, Dad!" Mary-Kate groaned. "Do you have to?"

"Hey," Kevin said. "You're going to a dance and I'm taking pictures."

He snapped a few more, and the flash went off in Mary-Kate's face.

"Now I'll be too blind to even *recognize* Jeremy at the dance!" she muttered.

"Don't worry, I'll steer you toward him," Ashley said.

"I can't get over this," Kevin said, staring at them both proudly. He folded his arms across his chest and gave them a warm smile. "It seems like only yesterday . . ."

Ashley and Mary-Kate exchanged glances. They knew what was coming.

"When we were in diapers," Mary-Kate finished her father's sentence.

"Yes," Ashley chimed in. "We were so cute, weren't we, Dad?"

Kevin made a face. "Yeah," he joked. "You were adorable. Then you learned to *talk.*"

"Ha, ha," Ashley said, glancing at the clock. "Come on, Dad. We'd better go. And don't forget the rules. Don't talk to us at the dance, unless we talk to you, all right? Don't spend the whole night gobbling down the refreshments. And *don't* watch us! Try to find a dark corner and just go stand in it, okay?"

"Yes, your royal highness," Kevin said, bowing at the waist. "Anything else?"

"Whatever you do, *don't* dance!" Mary-Kate exclaimed.

Ashley nodded. "And you'll need to drop us off a block from the school—so we won't be seen with you. It's nothing personal, Dad," she added quickly.

"It's just that it's uncool to be seen with a parent at a school dance."

"Fine," Kevin joked. "How about if I just slow down so you can leap out?"

He thinks that's funny, Mary-Kate thought, *but it isn't. If I don't calm down, I might seriously consider jumping from a moving car!*

Mary-Kate took a few deep breaths to steady her nerves.

Liking a boy was harder than she thought it would be.

Much harder.

She rode all the way to school bouncing her feet nervously. Going through the steps.

Basic step. Rock-step. Twist, twist, twirl . . .

I hope he doesn't ask me to dance the minute we walk in, she thought. *I need a few seconds to get used to the music.*

Five, six, seven, eight, she counted, rehearsing the moves over and over again.

She was so busy practicing the dance steps in her head that she didn't even notice what was happening.

Her dad was stopping the car. She and Ashley were walking into school. Now they were at the top of the school steps—and walking through the door.

Then all of a sudden, they were walking into the gym.

Here I am—at the dance! Mary-Kate thought excitedly.

"There's Jennifer," Ashley said. "Let's go stand with her until Jeremy asks you to dance."

"Sounds like a plan," Mary-Kate agreed.

As they crossed the gym, Mary-Kate saw Max and Brian on the dance floor.

"Wow, look at them," Mary-Kate said, nudging Ashley. "They're hanging out with *eighth* graders!"

"That's because Max and Brian will actually *dance*," Ashley reported. "For the first time in their lives, they're in demand."

Mary-Kate laughed. It was true. Not too many guys were dancing. They probably didn't know how.

Which was what made Jeremy seem so amazing! And scary.

A moment later, a boy from their English class came up and asked Ashley to dance. Mary-Kate watched as her sister and the guy hit the dance floor.

The song was a swing dance, but most kids were just doing regular dance moves. Some girls were dancing with other girls. A lot of the dancers were in groups of guys and girls together. They were all just bopping along in one big happy crowd.

Mary-Kate sort of wanted to join them. But she was waiting for Jeremy to ask her to dance.

She scanned the gym, searching for him. Finally she spotted him in the far corner. He was hanging out with a bunch of his friends from the wrestling team.

Her eyes caught his, and he half smiled.

Here he comes! Mary-Kate thought. Her heart started to pound in double time.

But Jeremy didn't make a move. He just gave a little nod, and then looked away.

Wow, Mary-Kate wondered. *What was that all about?*

Maybe he's changed his mind about dancing with me. Or maybe . . . maybe he doesn't like me!

"Have you seen Jeremy?" Jennifer asked, twirling off the dance floor. She grabbed Mary-Kate's arm. "Has he asked you to dance yet?"

"Uh, not yet," Mary-Kate started to say.

But Jennifer twirled back onto the dance floor before she even heard the answer.

This is embarrassing, Mary-Kate thought. *Everyone's waiting for Jeremy to ask me to dance!*

For the next half hour, Mary-Kate tried to pretend she was having a good time. She talked with girls she hardly knew. And she smiled whenever her dad looked over at her from the refreshment table.

But inside she was growing more and more miserable.

Even when she glanced over at Jeremy—*twice*—and he smiled—*twice*—she was unhappy.

Why wasn't he asking her to dance?

Maybe he's waiting for the right song, Mary-Kate thought hopefully.

"Hey, Mary-Kate," a voice beside her said. "Want to dance?"

Mary-Kate caught her breath. She whirled around with a huge smile. But it was only Max.

"Oh, hi, Max," she said glumly.

He was sweating from dancing so much, but he smiled and held out his hand to her.

"Want to dance, Mary-Kate?" he repeated.

Dance? Mary-Kate thought. *With a guy I can totally whip at one-on-one basketball? I don't think so.*

Besides, what if she was dancing with Max when Jeremy came over to ask her?

"Uh, no thanks, Max," Mary-Kate said. "I'm, uh, waiting to talk to someone."

"Whatever," Max said with a shrug. He hurried back to join the others on the dance floor.

Mary-Kate glanced over to see if Jeremy had noticed her talking to Max.

Oh, no—now he was talking to Marcie!

I'll die if he dances with Marcie instead of me! Mary-Kate thought. She watched them out of the corner of her eye.

But soon Marcie drifted back to her friends, and Mary-Kate let out her breath.

A minute later Ashley came zipping off the dance floor.

"Well?" she asked Mary-Kate. "What's he *waiting* for?"

"Who knows?" Mary-Kate said with a shrug. "This is the third swing dance they've played, and he hasn't moved."

"Maybe he's afraid you're not a good enough dancer," Ashley suggested. "Come on—let's show him what he's missing."

Mary-Kate let her sister pull her out into the middle of the crowd. Then the two of them went into the moves Carrie had taught them.

Basic step, rock-step, rock-step . . .

This is fun! Mary-Kate thought, forgetting about Jeremy for a minute. She and Ashley cuddled and twirled, spinning in perfect time to the song.

"Oh my gosh, he's looking at you!" Ashley squealed as the two of them danced on.

Mary-Kate glanced over to Jeremy's corner. He sort of nodded—for the fourth time that night.

"He nodded at you," Ashley declared. "I saw it. He definitely nodded."

"Maybe I should wave," Mary-Kate said.

"Are you crazy?" Ashley said, her eyes opening wide. "You don't wave to a nod."

See? Mary-Kate thought. *I'm not cut out for this! I'm in way over my head.*

"What do I do?" Mary-Kate pleaded nervously.

"Just give him a smile and a hair flip," Ashley advised.

"Okay," Mary-Kate said. "I can do that."

She spun around on the dance floor and flashed a big smile at Jeremy. Then she threw in the hair flip, just like Ashley said.

"How was that?" Mary-Kate asked.

"Perfect," Ashley replied.

"Good," Mary-Kate gasped. "But I think I just swallowed my gum!"

When the song was over, Mary-Kate and Ashley moved to the sidelines and joined their group of friends.

"You looked amazing out there," Jennifer complimented Mary-Kate. "I don't get it—what's Jeremy waiting for?"

"Don't ask me!" Mary-Kate answered. "I can't read his mind."

"He's been checking you out all night," Jennifer went on. "And he hasn't been with anyone else. So why won't he ask you to dance?"

"If he's going to make a move, he'd better do it soon," Ashley said. "The dance is almost over."

"Really?" Mary-Kate's head snapped toward the clock.

Whoa! Ashley was right. The time had flown by, and the dance would end in another half hour.

All at once, Mary-Kate started to get mad.

"That's it," she said. She was totally fed up. "I've spent three days learning to swing dance. And three hours getting dressed. So I'm getting at least three *minutes* of dancing out of him!"

She flipped her hair one more time, to get up the nerve to do what she was planning to do.

Then she spun on her heels to face Jeremy.

"Whoa," Jennifer gasped. *"You're* going to ask *him*?"

Mary-Kate didn't wait for her friends to take a vote. Her mind was made up. She marched straight across the gym to where Jeremy was standing.

"Hey, Jeremy," she said, her heart pounding.

"Hi, Mary-Kate," he said.

"So," Mary-Kate blurted out, "you feel like swing dancing with me?"

Jeremy didn't even take a second to think about it. He just gave her his answer. Straight out.

"Nah," he said. "I don't think so."

Mary-Kate felt as though she had just been punched in the stomach. She had been totally, utterly, completely rejected!

CHAPTER ELEVEN

"Well? What did he say?" Ashley asked eagerly.

Mary-Kate could hardly speak. She felt as if her head was spinning off.

She had just asked the first boy she ever liked to dance with her.

And he said no.

He didn't even bother coming up with an excuse.

"What did he say?" Ashley repeated.

"He turned me down," Mary-Kate answered.

Ashley gasped in shock. "Are you kidding? How could he?" she asked.

"He made it seem pretty easy." Mary-Kate spoke in a small voice.

Ashley gave Mary-Kate's arm a squeeze. "I'm

sorry," she said. "Wow. I can't believe he had the nerve to do that. I mean, he practically promised to swing dance with you, didn't he?"

Mary-Kate just shrugged.

Let's not keep talking about it, she thought. *Or else this lump in my throat is going to get even larger. And I'll start crying.*

Mary-Kate took a deep breath and glanced toward the refreshment table. Her dad was there, serving punch to some eighth-grade girls.

Suddenly Mary-Kate wasn't sorry her dad was a chaperone. At least he was a friendly face.

"It's no big deal," Mary-Kate told Ashley. "Just forget it. I'm going to get something to eat."

"No way," Ashley said. "I will not forget it. I'm going to have a talk with Jeremy *myself*!"

"Ashley—no!" Mary-Kate called.

But she was too late. Ashley was already heading off toward Jeremy's corner.

Oh, well, Mary-Kate thought. *Let her talk to him if she wants to. What good will it do?*

The refreshment table was near the door. Mary-Kate made her way over to it and stood quietly, picking at some chips. Her dad poured a cup of punch for someone. Then he moved closer to Mary-Kate.

"Is it okay if I say hi?" he asked in a whisper.

Mary-Kate shrugged. "Sure."

Kevin peered at her. "What's the matter?" he asked.

"I just asked this guy I like to dance, and he said no," Mary-Kate answered.

Kevin leaned across the table, reaching out to give Mary-Kate a hug. "Oh, honey . . ." he started to say.

"Dad!" Mary-Kate scolded, backing away. "Please don't make a scene—everyone will notice!"

"Sorry," Kevin said, quickly backing up. "Forgot the rules."

"I'm ready to leave any time," Mary-Kate mumbled. "Whenever you are."

Kevin tilted his head and gazed at his daughter. "Don't let one guy spoil your whole evening," he said. "You can still dance with Max or Brian . . ."

Mary-Kate rolled her eyes. "*Dad*," she said. She nibbled at another chip, but could barely swallow it. "The sooner we leave, the better," she muttered.

Kevin started to nod. But then all at once she saw his face light up. He stared at someone behind Mary-Kate's back.

"On the other hand, why don't you think that over and get back to me?" Kevin said.

Mary-Kate whirled around to see what he was looking at.

Ashley was coming across the room—with Jeremy behind her!

She's practically dragging him over here to talk to me! Mary-Kate thought.

"Okay, tell her what you told me," Ashley ordered Jeremy sternly.

Mary-Kate felt her face turning red.

"Ashley, what are you doing?" She glared at her sister.

"Jeremy's got something to say," Ashley explained. She gave him a hard stare. "Go ahead. And remember—I'll be right over there watching."

Then Ashley backed off and left Jeremy standing face-to-face with Mary-Kate.

He is so cute, Mary-Kate thought. Her heart started pounding again. *I just hope he doesn't say anything horrible. Because I can't take any more bad news tonight.*

She held her breath and watched Jeremy. He looked totally uncomfortable.

"Uh, Mary-Kate," he began slowly. "You know how I said I only did swing dancing?"

Mary-Kate nodded.

"Well, I lied. The truth is, I can't dance."

Can't dance? Mary-Kate thought, feeling confused.

"I don't get it," she said. "Then why did you say you were a great swing dancer?"

"Because I didn't want to admit that I can't dance at all. And I never thought *you'd* know how," he explained. "Not too many kids do."

"Well, I *didn't* know how until three days ago!" Mary-Kate blurted out.

Jeremy's eyes opened wide. "You mean you learned just because of me?" he asked.

"Uh, yeah," she admitted. "It certainly looks that way, doesn't it?"

"Wow," Jeremy said. He smiled at her.

Then he glanced over at the dance floor. A romantic slow song was playing. Couples were dancing close together.

"You know, *that* doesn't look too hard," he said. "Do you think you could teach me?"

He wants to slow dance? Mary-Kate thought. *With me? Wow!*

Mary-Kate shrugged. "I could try," she said, feeling happy for the first time that night.

"Great," Jeremy said. He followed her onto the dance floor.

Mary-Kate put her left arm on Jeremy's shoulder. Then she took his right hand.

"Now all you do is . . . dance!" Mary-Kate explained.

Jeremy put his hand on the back of Mary-Kate's waist. The two of them swayed in time to the music. Jeremy's head was bent so close to hers, they were practically touching.

Wow, Mary-Kate thought. *Why did I spend so much time learning to swing dance? This is so much better!*

When the song was over, Jeremy stood there as if he didn't know what to do next. A swing dance song came on.

"Uh-oh," he said, blushing. "I'm definitely not ready to do *that* right now. Not here in front of everybody!"

Mary-Kate laughed. "I know what you mean," she said. "It involves a lot of falling down at first."

"You want to get some punch?" he suggested, nodding toward the refreshment table.

"Sure," Mary-Kate agreed. *Anything to stay with you!* she thought.

Then she glanced at the table to see if her dad was there. But Kevin was gone. She and Jeremy walked over to the table. They each picked up a cup of punch. Then they turned around to watch the dancers.

"Oh, *no!*" Mary-Kate blurted out when she saw what was happening.

Everyone in the whole gym had formed a semicircle around two dancers. They were swing dancing wildly, tearing up the place. People clapped and cheered them on.

The dancers were her dad and Carrie!

"Wow!" Jeremy said. "They're great!"

"Yeah," Mary-Kate agreed. "They're great—and they're history! Give me a moment, Jeremy—I'll be right back."

Quickly she found Ashley in the crowd. "We've got to do something," Mary-Kate said urgently.

Ashley gave their father the "cut" sign by running her finger across her throat.

But Kevin and Carrie kept dancing.

"Way to go, Mr. Burke," Max shouted.

"Yeah, Carrie!" Jennifer cried.

"You know, Mary-Kate," Ashley whispered, "I guess Dad's not such a bad dancer after all."

"Everyone actually seems to like them," Mary-Kate agreed. "You've got to admit—Dad may be weird, but he's got style!"

Finally Kevin and Carrie stopped dancing. They went back to the refreshment table.

"I'm glad that's over," Mary-Kate said to her sister. "Where did Carrie come from, anyway?"

"She said she might stop by, remember?" Ashley said.

"At least she wasn't dancing with Dad the whole night," Mary-Kate said. "Anyhow, nothing could ruin tonight for me. I'm having a fabulous time. Thanks for talking to Jeremy."

"No problem," Ashley replied. "That's my job—matchmaker."

Mary-Kate smiled.

"Besides," Ashley went on. "Tonight's your night, so enjoy it. Because after this, you're going to be getting sick, remember?"

"Sick? Oh, yeah," Mary-Kate said.

"And then it's *my* turn to have my dream come true," Ashley said. "At the fashion shoot on Monday."

Mary-Kate's face fell. She wasn't in the mood to pretend to get sick. If she missed school, she'd miss seeing Jeremy!

Besides, the deal was off. Ashley didn't teach her to swing dance—Carrie did!

Mary-Kate opened her mouth to say something. Then she remembered—it was Ashley who got Jeremy to dance with her! So she owed Ashley big-time.

Oh, well, Mary-Kate decided. *I won't think about any of that now.*

"So enjoy yourself!" Ashley repeated. "Tonight's *your* big night. And on Monday, the fun starts for *me!*

CHAPTER TWELVE

"Maybe I should plan what to wear tomorrow," Ashley said to herself on Sunday.

For once, Ashley couldn't *wait* for the school week to arrive. The sooner she went back to school, the sooner the fashion shoot would start.

She knew the Fashion Van would provide all the clothes for the modeling session. But still she didn't want to show up looking bad.

If I want to be treated like a model, I've got to dress like a model, Ashley decided.

Maybe I should wear my lavender slip dress with the flowered top, she thought. *Or my sparkly blue skirt.*

Then she remembered the truth—*Real Teen* magazine had picked Mary-Kate for the photo shoot because she had a "natural" look.

Hmmm, she thought as she climbed the stairs to her room. *Maybe I should dress like Mary-Kate?*

Not!

As she reached the door to their room, she heard Mary-Kate inside, talking to herself.

Ashley walked on tiptoe. She peeked in and listened.

Mary-Kate was standing in front of their full-length mirror holding *Real Teen* magazine. She glanced first at the models on the page and then at herself in the mirror. Then back to the magazine.

Finally she struck a pose.

Wow, Ashley thought. *She's pretending to model!*

"That's so beautiful," Mary-Kate said to herself in a phony accent. "Now turn and give me a pouty look, Mary-Kate."

Mary-Kate pursed her lips together and gazed into the mirror.

"The camera loves you," Mary-Kate cooed as she went on posing. "Absolutely loves you."

Ashley didn't want to just stand there spying. So she stepped into the room and cleared her throat.

"What are you doing?" she asked her sister.

Mary-Kate jumped. "Nothing!" she said, dropping the magazine.

"Come on, Mary-Kate," Ashley said. "I *know* when someone's modeling in front of a mirror. I've been doing it since I could stand!"

Mary-Kate blushed. "I just kind of wanted to see what it would be like to be a model," she explained.

"Why?" Ashley demanded. "I mean, you've never cared about that stuff. Everybody knows that."

Mary-Kate turned away.

"Well, maybe everybody's wrong," she said. "Maybe sometimes I like the same things you do. I just don't talk about them a whole lot. "

"Wow," Ashley said. "So you really *are* interested in clothes, and boys, and schoolwork, and math . . ."

"*Not* math," Mary-Kate shot back. "But clothes?" She shrugged. "I like to look good, too."

Ashley thought a moment. "If you really wanted to do the fashion shoot," she said, "why didn't you just tell me?"

"Oh, right. And when would I have done that?" Mary-Kate asked. "When you were asking me to sprain my ankle? Or when you suggested I throw myself down a flight of stairs?"

"I guess I was desperate," Ashley admitted.

"More like possessed!" Mary-Kate said.

Ashley laughed.

"Besides," Mary-Kate went on, "I was really grateful to you for what you did at the dance on Friday. I had a great time with Jeremy." She smiled. "And he called this morning to ask me about science homework. So I guess I figured that . . . that I *have* to let you do the modeling gig."

"No," Ashley said, shaking her head. "You don't *have* to."

Ashley and Mary-Kate's eyes locked.

Ashley knew what she *should* do. She should let Mary-Kate have the modeling job back. After all, it was actually Mary-Kate's in the first place!

But Ashley really wanted it.

She took a deep breath.

"You know what?" she finally said to her sister. "They picked you, not me. *You* do the shoot tomorrow."

"No, no." Mary-Kate shook her head. "I gave it to you."

"And I'm giving it back," Ashley insisted. "It sounds like it means as much to you as it does to me."

Mary-Kate shook her head again. "No, I couldn't take it away from you," she argued. But she didn't sound as if she really meant it.

Boy, she's making this hard on me! Ashley thought. *What does she want me to do—beg?*

"This is the last time I'm offering," Ashley warned.

"Okay!" Mary-Kate said quickly. "I'll do it!"

"Good," Ashley said.

Mary-Kate raced over and gave Ashley a big hug. "Thanks, Ashley," she said. "I hope I'll be okay."

"You'll be great," Ashley reassured her. "A really great model."

And I'll be a great actress, she thought. *That way, no one will know how jealous I am!*

CHAPTER THIRTEEN

"Do I look okay?" Mary-Kate asked for the fifteenth time.

Both girls stood at the kitchen counter the next morning trying to eat breakfast before the big fashion shoot.

Mary-Kate looked excited and nervous.

Ashley's stomach was full of butterflies, too. She wasn't sure how she was going to get through the day.

Maybe I just won't watch the fashion shoot, Ashley thought. *That way I won't have to think about how it could have been me.*

"Do I?" Mary-Kate repeated. "Do I look all right?"

Ashley nodded and took another bite of her blueberry muffin. "You look great. And don't forget—they're going to fix your hair and put on your makeup. And *they're* bringing all the clothes."

"And I get to keep them after the shoot—right?" Mary-Kate asked.

"Right," Ashley answered. She grinned. "And the good thing is—even if you don't like them, they'll fit *me!*"

Mary-Kate picked blueberries out of her muffin and ate them.

"I'm so nervous," she admitted. "I don't think I could do this without you, Ashley. You'll be there, won't you? I mean, for moral support?"

"Uh, sure. I guess," Ashley replied. "If they let me out of class."

"You're the best, Ashley," Mary-Kate said. She gave her sister a big hug.

Ashley stared at her muffin. Somehow she didn't want to eat any more.

"Okay, girls, time to go," Kevin announced.

Mary-Kate went to get her backpack. Kevin looked over at Ashley.

He's reading my mind, Ashley realized. *He knows how disappointed I am.*

Kevin came over and gave Ashley a pat on the

back. "I'm really proud of you for being there for your sister," he said. "And not letting your own feelings get in the way."

"Thanks, Dad," Ashley said. She wrinkled her nose. "But I still wish this day was over."

By the time they reached school, Ashley had her brave face in place.

Smile, she told herself. *Pretending* was what modeling was all about, after all. It was about looking happy, or sad, or serious—even when you *weren't* in the mood.

So this was going to be good practice.

Inside the school the Fashion Van team was already at work. Two assistants were busy setting up lights in the hallway near some lockers. Tara James was talking with a magazine editor about the clothes. A makeup artist had set up a mirror in an empty classroom. Her brushes and makeup were spread out on a big table.

And the first-floor girls' rest room had a sign on the door: DRESSING ROOM: MODELS ONLY!

"Wow," Mary-Kate cried. "This is so cool!"

Ashley found Jennifer in a crowd of kids who were hanging around watching.

"They're going to be sorry they didn't pick us," Jennifer muttered.

"No, they won't," Ashley said. "Mary-Kate's going to do a *great* job."

A minute later Mary-Kate was swept up in all the activity. Tara James took her into the dressing room with a pile of clothes over her arm. Ashley and Jennifer watched from across the hall.

"Did you see that?" Jennifer cried. "That black-and-red sweater outfit! The one Tara was carrying!"

"No. What about it?" Ashley asked.

"It's exactly like the one you're wearing today!" Jennifer announced. "See what I mean? We were born to do this. They've made a huge mistake."

"Look," Ashley said firmly. "We *didn't* get picked, and there's nothing we can do about that. I'm not going to spend the whole day being unhappy—not if I can possibly help it. So let's just drop it, okay?"

Jennifer shrugged. "Whatever," she muttered.

Finally Mary-Kate came out of the dressing room wearing a pair of blue plaid flared pants and a short blue top.

Ashley watched as the photographer, a guy named Darren, positioned Mary-Kate in front of the lockers. Then he spent about twenty minutes adjusting his lights.

Finally he was ready to take some pictures.

"Okay, Mary-Kate," he said, smiling at her. "Put one hand on the locker and look this way. Great! You're a natural."

Click. Flash. Click-click-click.

He took a dozen pictures a minute.

She does *look good*, Ashley thought, feeling proud of her sister. *No wonder they picked Mary-Kate. She is really doing an awesome job!*

"Now this way, Mary-Kate," Darren called. "Turn your head, chin up a little, great!"

Click. Flash. Click. Flash.

"Okay, one more for me," Darren said at the end of each pose.

Mary-Kate tossed her head back and gave him a big smile.

"Perfect!" Darren called. "Reload."

"How do I do that?" Mary-Kate asked, sounding worried.

"Not you—me," Darren explained with a laugh. "It's time for my assistants to reload my film. You get to take a break."

Mary-Kate raced over to Ashley, who was waiting for her off to the side.

"How am I doing?" she asked Ashley excitedly.

"Great!" Ashley reassured her. "You look absolutely fabulous!"

Mary-Kate giggled, her eyes sparkling. "And I'm just getting started!" she announced.

"Whoa!" Ashley shot back. "I think I've created a monster!"

Mary-Kate grabbed Ashley's hands and gave them a squeeze. "Thanks for everything. You're the best."

Ashley started to answer when she noticed Darren, the photographer, staring at her. His eyes popped open.

"What am I seeing?" he asked, strolling toward them. "Double?" He looked from Mary-Kate to Ashley and back again. "I don't recognize you from the tryouts," he said to Ashley.

Tara James gazed at Ashley from the sidelines. "No, neither do I," she said.

I must have looked really different with makeup and fancy clothes, Ashley thought. "I, um . . ." she began.

"Hey," Mary-Kate said quickly. "How would you like to take pictures of both of us?"

Before Darren could answer, Mary-Kate grabbed Ashley by the hand. She pulled her over to the lockers where Mary-Kate had been posing.

"This is your lucky day," Mary-Kate said to Darren. She turned to Ashley. "Let's show them what we can do!"

"Are you sure it's all right?" Ashley whispered to Mary-Kate. "I mean, nobody's asked me!"

"What a great idea!" Darren exclaimed. He turned to Ashley. "You're on."

"Yes!" Ashley said, bursting with excitement. *This is what I've been waiting for—forever!* she thought. *This is the best day of my whole life!*

Instantly the two of them struck a pose. They put their cheeks side by side. Each girl put one hand on her hip. They looked like a reflection in a mirror.

"Fantastic!" Darren called, snapping one picture after another.

Click-click-click. Flash-flash-flash.

"Keep going!" Darren called as Mary-Kate and Ashley struck other poses. "Talk about talent. The two of you ought to think about doing this professionally!"

Click-click-click.

"Now give him a hair flip," Ashley coached under her breath.

Mary-Kate did as Ashley suggested. Together the two of them flipped their hair and struck a cool pose.

Click-flash-click-flash-click!

"She's even wearing the right outfit!" Tara commented from off to the side. "We needed that red-

and-black sweater outfit for the magazine layout, anyway."

Mary-Kate nudged Ashley. "See? Your fabulous fashion sense came through for you, after all!"

Ashley grinned. From the corner of her eye, she could see Jennifer watching her. She looked green with envy. *Poor Jennifer!* Ashley thought. *Maybe she can model next time—if* Real Teen *does an evening wear issue!*

By the time the fashion shoot was over, Ashley was tired. But it was a happy kind of tired. Modeling was even more fun than she thought it would be.

And it went so well that she was sure it wouldn't be her last shoot.

"You were both great," Tara said, as she handed Ashley an armload of clothes to take home. "Thanks for showing us that two models are better than one."

"Right," Mary-Kate chimed in. "Especially when they're two of a kind!"

Mary-Kate & Ashley's Scrapbook

One day at school Mary-Kate and I heard the most exciting news ever. The Fashion Van was coming to pick models for the next issue of *Real Teen* magazine! I was sure they would pick me.

Mary-Kate had some news of her own. She had
a crush on a boy named Jeremy. I wanted her to
ask Jeremy to the dance on Friday. The only
problem was—Jeremy liked to swing dance. And
Mary-Kate didn't know how. . . .

Then came the real surprise. Mary-Kate got
picked to model—and I didn't! I begged her to
change places with me.

So we made a deal. I would teach Mary-Kate to swing dance—and she would let me model. Except that I don't really know how to swing dance, so Carrie agreed to help.

The big night came. Mary-Kate asked
Jeremy to dance. And he said no! I made
him confess—he didn't know how to
swing dance after all.

Finally Mary-Kate got to slow dance with Jeremy. And I showed off my swing moves myself!

Everything was great.
And on Monday it would
be my turn to model.
But then Mary-Kate
started thinking that
modeling might be kind
of cool after all.

Luckily, the *Real Teen* people thought that two models were better than one. Now Mary-Kate and I can both say: "My Sister the Supermodel!"

PSST! Take a sneak peek
at

Two's a Crowd

"Dad, can you give us a hand in here, please?" Ashley called out of the bedroom door.

"Sure, Ashley," Kevin called back from the hall. "I'll be right there."

But when Kevin appeared at the door he froze. He stepped into the room and looked around.

"Whoa!" Kevin gasped.

Ashley turned away from the closet she was dusting. She knew her father would come upstairs sooner or later.

"Something wrong, Dad?" she asked, twirling her feather duster. "You look like you just saw a ghost."

"You bet there's something wrong," Kevin cried. He pointed to Mary-Kate, who was loading a cardboard box with trophies. "Mary-Kate is packing boxes. And you're dusting out Mary-Kate's side of the closet. Can someone please tell me what's going on in here?"

"Mary-Kate is moving up to the attic," Ashley said.

"Excuse me," Mary-Kate said. She placed her hands on her hips. "I like to refer to it as the penthouse!"

Ashley rolled her eyes. Mary-Kate had always called the attic the rec room. Now it was the penthouse. La-dee-da!

"Whatever." Ashley waved her hand over the closet. "All I know is that I'm going to have closet space for a change. Oh thank you, Universe!"

Kevin ran his hand through his hair and sighed.

"Mary-Kate, Ashley," he said. "I know you two had a little fight. But can't you settle it some other way? Like draw a line down the middle of the room?"

"Oh, Dad!"Ashley rolled her eyes. "We did that when we were just kids. Besides, we've got it all worked out."

"And it's all here in writing!" Mary-Kate said, holding up a piece of paper.

Kevin took the sheet of paper. He looked at it and blinked. "A custody agreement?"

"You and Carrie told us to work things out." Ashley shrugged. "So we did. We divided all the stuff we share right down the middle."

"I get the Walkman every even day," Mary-Kate explained.

"And I get the curling iron every odd day," Ashley said.

Mary-Kate snickered. "Every day you style your hair is an odd day, Ashley."

Ashley glared at Mary-Kate. "That does it!" she cried. She turned to her father and planted her hands on her hips. "I want Mary-Kate's bed out of here by tonight!"

"Tonight?" Kevin cried.

"Tonight!" Ashley repeated.

"Fine with me," Mary-Kate said. She picked up an armload of rolled-up posters and stomped out of the room.

"Mary-Kate," Kevin called, running after her. "Wait!"

When Ashley was alone, she looked around the room. Without Mary-Kate's sports posters and piles of clothes, the room seemed practically empty.

All this space—just for me! Ashley thought. *I won't miss Mary-Kate's junk at all. And I certainly won't miss Mary-Kate!*

Two Times the Fun!
Two Times the Excitement!
Two Times the Adventure!

Check Out All Eight *You're Invited* Video Titles...

... And All Four Feature-Length Movies!

And Look for Mary-Kate & Ashley's
Adventure Video Series.

DUALSTAR VIDEO

**Load up
the one-horse
open sleigh.
Mary-Kate and Ashley's
Christmas Album
is on the way.**

It doesn't matter if you live around the corner...
or around the world....
If you are a fan of Mary-Kate and Ashley Olsen,
you should be a member of

Mary-Kate + Ashley's Fun Club™

Here's what you get
Our Funzine™
An autographed color photo
Two black and white individual photos
A full sized color poster
An official Fun Club™ membership card
A Fun Club™ School folder
Two special Fun Club™ surprises
Fun Club™ Collectible Catalog
Plus a Fun Club™ box to keep everything in.

To join Mary-Kate + Ashley's Fun Club™, fill out the form below
and send it along with

U.S. Residents	$17.00
Canadian Residents	$22.00 (US Funds only)
International Residents	$27.00 (US Funds only)

Mary-Kate + Ashley's Fun Club™
859 Hollywood Way, Suite 275
Burbank, CA 91505

Name:_____

Address:_____

City:_____ St:_____ Zip:_____

Phone: (_____) _____

E-Mail:_____

Check us out on the web at
www.marykateandashley.com